Lily's Pesky Plant

This edition published by Parragon in 2011

Parragon
Queen Street House
4 Queen Street
Bath, BA1 1HE, UK

ISBN 978-1-4454-2260-2

Printed in China.

Lily's Pesky Plant

WRITTEN BY

Kirsten Larsen

ILLUSTRATED BY

Judith Holmes Clarke
&
The Disney Storybook Artists

Bath • New York • Singapore • Hong Kong • Cologne • Delhi
Melbourne • Amsterdam • Johannesburg • Auckland • Shenzhen

Early one morning, Lily woke to the sound of birds chirping in the topmost branches of the Home Tree. She climbed out of bed and dressed quickly. Then she headed down to the tearoom.

Lily had a cup of lemongrass tea and a slice of poppy-seed cake for breakfast. The moment her plate and cup were empty, she pushed them aside and flew off to her garden.

Lily's garden was just two frog leaps beyond the Home Tree. All the fairies agreed that it was one of the nicest places in Pixie Hollow. On one side of her garden was a hedge of raspberry bushes. On the other side, a wild rosebush sweetly scented the air. Everywhere bright red and orange poppies sprang from the ground. Clusters of Queen Anne's lace and lilac made pleasant groves where a fairy could sit and think. And throughout the garden, sweet clover sprouted in fairy-sized beds; perfect for taking naps in.

As soon as Lily got to her garden,

she called out, "Bumble!" A large bee zipped out of the flowers and flew up to her. Bumble always followed Lily as she took care of her plants.

When she was done making the rounds in her garden, Lily lay down on a patch of soft moss to watch the grass grow.

Bumble was buzzing around the buttercups in the corner of the garden, and Lily was lying nearby, watching a very slow race between two blades of grass, when a voice suddenly interrupted her thoughts.

"I say, what a funny thing!"

Lily looked up. A tall fairy was standing over her.

"Hello, Iris," said Lily, sitting up. "What's so funny?"

"Why, just look at your buttercups."

Lily looked. She didn't see anything funny about them.

"They're the biggest I've ever seen!" Iris exclaimed. "You ought to call them butter-*bowls* instead. Of course, they're nothing like the buttercups I used to grow," Iris went on. "They were as big as soup pots and yellow as the sun."

Like Lily, Iris was a garden-talent fairy. She had once had her own garden, but it was so long ago that no one could remember what it had been like. Then Iris had begun writing her

plant book. Now, she claimed she was much too busy to do any real gardening.

Iris plopped down on a spotted red toadstool and flipped open the birch bark cover of her book. "Anyway, Lily," Iris said, "I've come because I'm worried about your snapdragons. Now, don't get me wrong. They seem perfectly healthy and strong. But when I went to take a peek at their petals the other day, one snapped at me!"

"They're snapdragons, Iris," Lily pointed out patiently. "It's their nature to be cranky."

"Well, I know a thing or two about how to keep snapdragons

from snapping," Iris said. She tapped the page she'd opened to. "Here, I'll read it to you. 'A Cure for Snappish Snapdragons, by Iris.'"

As Iris read on, Lily's toes began to wiggle impatiently. Suddenly, she blurted out, "Actually, Iris, I was just about to leave."

It wasn't true, and Lily wasn't quite sure why she'd said it. She knew Iris only meant to be helpful. But on this particular day, Lily just didn't feel like listening to Iris.

"Oh. Okay, then. Another time." Iris looked disappointed, and Lily felt a little pang of regret. But it was too late to take it back now.

"Yes, another time. See you, Iris," Lily said. She rose into the air and flew off into the forest.

When she was just out of sight from the garden, Lily landed near the roots of an old oak tree.

"I'll just go for a short walk," she told herself. "Then I'll go back." She figured Iris would have moved to someone else's garden by then.

Lily took off her shoes and walked along the forest floor. She liked the feeling of the damp soil between her toes.

Suddenly, something crashed through the leaves over her head. Lily

gasped and flew for cover between the
roots of a nearby tree. Trembling, she
peered out from behind the root and
scanned the forest.

Then Lily saw something that
made her gasp again. In the spot
where she had just been standing lay
a strange seed.

At least, Lily thought it was a seed. She had never seen anything quite like it before. It was as big as a chestnut and a pearly white colour.

Lily flew over and landed next to the strange object. She touched it with her fingertips. The surface felt cool and smooth, like a sea-polished rock.

Now Lily was sure it was a seed. Her gardening instincts told her there was

life inside it – the sleeping life of a
plant waiting to grow.

"But where did it come from?" Lily
asked aloud.

Just then, she heard a loud
chittering sound above her. She
looked up. A squirrel was chattering
at her from a branch overhead.

Lily looked back down at the seed. For once, she wished she were an animal-talent fairy. Then she could talk to the squirrel and ask him where the mysterious seed had come from.

Suddenly, something occurred to her. "I'll plant it!" she exclaimed.

She reached down to pick it up. Clutching her treasure against her chest, Lily rose into the air and flew in the direction of her garden.

Back at her garden, Lily found Iris still sitting on the toadstool, right where she had left her.

"Oh, Lily, you're back already," said Iris.

Lily no longer felt annoyed with Iris. She was much too excited about her find. Gently, Lily placed the big seed on the ground.

"What an amazing seed!" Iris cried. "Whatever is it?"

"You don't know?" Lily asked. "I was hoping you would. I found it in the forest just now. I've never seen one before."

Iris squinted closely at the seed. Then she made a note in her book. She began to draw a picture of the seed next to it.

"Hi, Lily. Hi, Iris. What is that? It's so lovely!" said a friendly voice. Rani, a water-talent fairy with long, blonde hair, walked over to them.

"Hi, Rani," said Lily. "It's some kind of seed. We're not sure what. I found it today in the—"

"—beach cove?" Rani asked.

"No, the forest," said Lily.

"Oh. It's just that it reminds me of a shell," Rani said, squatting down to admire the seed.

"Well," said Lily, "there's only one way to find out what it is." She picked up a shovel and drove the tip into the ground.

Iris looked up from her book. "You're going to plant it? Just like that?" she asked. "But you don't know how much sunlight it needs. Or how

CLOVER

much water. And what if it doesn't get along with the other flowers? And... and..."

Lily smiled. "I'm sure everything will be fine," she said.

3

A few days after she planted the seed, Lily was wrapping spider silk around some violets that had caught a chill when she was interrupted by a terrible racket.

Chomp! Chomp! Chomp!

The sound was coming from the other side of her garden. Lily hurried towards it.

There was Iris, sitting on top of a

strange contraption.

It had a seat and pedals. At the front of the machine was a set of huge metal jaws. Lily watched as Iris dumped a bucket of kitchen rubbish into the jaws. Then she put her feet on the pedals. As her legs moved, the metal jaws chewed up the rubbish.

Chomp! Chomp! Chomp!

"Just making a little food for our seed!" Iris shouted over the noise. "Only the best for our little plant." She went back to pedalling. Lily winced and put her hands over her ears.

Ever since Lily had planted the mysterious seed, Iris had come to

Lily's garden every day to check on it.

Iris finally finished mulching the rubbish. She picked up the bucket of plant food and set off in the direction of the seed. Lily went back to tending her violets.

Suddenly, Iris shrieked. "Look, Lily!" she said breathlessly. "It sprouted!"

Lily flew over to Iris. Sure enough, a small sprout was growing where they'd planted the mysterious seed.

"Oh, it's beautiful," Lily whispered.

In fact, the seedling wasn't beautiful at all. Its leaves were a sickly yellow colour. Its stem was covered with little spots.

"Vidia!" Iris called out to a fairy passing by. "Come look at our new little plant!"

Vidia stopped and looked at the seedling. She made a face. "Darlings, I've never seen anything so ugly in my life."

Lily ignored Vidia. "Iris, let's give it water," she said. "It looks as if it could use some."

Iris gave Vidia an angry glance. Then she picked up a bucket and hurried off to the stream.

"Lily, dear, how can you stand having her around all the time?" Vidia said. She glanced at Iris's back. "A garden fairy without a garden? How *sad*."

"She's better company than some fairies," Lily replied.

Vidia gave her a sugary smile. "Have fun with your little sprout," she said.

Rising into the air, Vidia put on a burst of speed and disappeared.

For the next several days, Lily and Iris carefully tended the plant. The seedling grew amazingly fast.

It grew uglier too. The small spots grew into big warts. Sticky sap dripped from its bark. It sprouted thin, droopy branches.

Lily didn't care. She could tell that the plant was happy, so she was happy too.

But the other fairies weren't quite so open-minded.

"Lily, come quick!" Tinker Bell said as she burst into the tearoom one morning. "A monster is attacking your buttercups!"

Lily dropped her teacup and the two fairies raced out of the Home Tree.

Outside Lily's garden, they paused

behind the rosebush. Tinker Bell
drew her dagger.

"There it is!" Tink
whispered, pointing.

Lily began to laugh. Then she flew
over and landed beside the "monster."

"Tink," she said between chuckles,
"meet my newest plant."

"That's a plant?" Tink said. She
peered up at its ugly branches. "What
kind is it?"

"I don't know. I found the seed in the
forest and planted it," Lily explained.

"Well, it's very... interesting,"
replied Tink.

Even the other garden fairies
were doubtful about Lily's plant.

"I've never seen anything like it," said Rosetta. "Are you sure you want such an ugly plant in your garden?"

"I'm sure," said Lily with a wide smile.

One morning, Lily noticed a strange odour in her garden. It smelled like rotten tomatoes and sour milk.

Lily began to walk through her garden, looking for the source of the stink.

When she came to a red spotted toadstool, Lily covered her nose with her hands. The smell was even stronger here.

Bumble, who had followed Lily, began to flit around nervously.

"What's gotten into you?" Lily said. Then she saw something that made

her forget all about Bumble. The mysterious plant had grown flowers.

Curious, Lily rose into the air until she was face-to-face with one of the flowers. She leaned forwards, closed her eyes and...

Ugh! Lily's wings froze in midflutter. She dropped out of the air and landed on the ground with a painful thud.

The horrible rotten-tomato smell was coming from the flowers.

"Lily, are you all right?" asked a muffled voice.

Lily looked up and saw Iris hurrying toward her. She was holding a leafkerchief over her nose and mouth. "I saw you fall," she told Lily.

"I'm all right," Lily replied. "Just surprised. I really wasn't expecting it to... stink so much!"

Iris held out a clean leafkerchief. Lily took it gratefully. Covering their noses, the two fairies stared up at the big, smelly flowers.

Suddenly, other voices piped up behind them. "What is that smell?"

A little group of fairies and sparrow men came flying toward them from the Home Tree. They were all wearing clothes pegs on their noses. They came to a sudden stop when they saw the giant flowers.

"How ugly!"

"That's what smells so bad."

"Lily, what in the name of Never Land is wrong with that plant?" asked Dulcie, a baking-talent fairy.

"Nothing," replied Lily.

"Well, can you do something about that smell? It's blowing in the windows of the tearoom," said a serving-talent sparrow man.

Lily looked around. Her eyes fell on a patch of lavender.

"I have an idea," she said. Hurrying over to her lavender, she picked a few pieces. She tucked a bit inside her leafkerchief and tied it around her nose and mouth like a mask. The lavender's sweetness covered up the bad smell.

She handed lavender to the other fairies. They pinned the flowers to their noses with the clothes pegs.

Just then, Lily heard a sound.

BZZZZZZZZZZZZZZZZZ...

Lily looked up. A black cloud seemed to be moving towards them across the sky.

BZZZZZZZZZZZZZZZZZ...

Lily looked closer. It wasn't a cloud at all. It was a huge swarm of wasps!

"Look out!" Lily cried.

The fairies leaped into the lavender for cover as the wasps dove toward them. But the wasps clustered around the flowers on the mysterious plant.

They seemed to like the strange smell.

"What do we do now?" Dulcie whispered to Lily.

Lily had no idea. They couldn't make a dash for the Home Tree, because they might get stung. But they couldn't hide in the lavender forever.

Just then, Lily heard a caw. She peeped out of the lavender and saw a large black shape swoop down from the sky. Another dark shape followed right behind it.

Ravens!

And riding on the ravens' backs, right between their wings, were fairies.

5

The ravens dove at the
wasps. The swarm began to break up.
The wasps were afraid of the huge
black birds.

Finally, the last wasp was gone. Lily
and the other fairies climbed out of
the lavender.

The ravens landed next to them.
On their backs were Beck and Fawn,
two animal-talent fairies.

"A scout saw the swarm go into your garden," Beck explained. "We thought there might be trouble, so we called the ravens."

"Is anyone hurt?" asked Fawn.

Iris burst into tears. "I nearly got stung!" she cried.

Fawn gently patted Iris's back to calm her down.

"Anyone else?" asked Beck.

The other fairies and sparrow men shook their heads. They were all scared, but no one had been harmed.

"Come on, Iris," Beck said. "Let's go back to the Home Tree. A cup of tea with honey will make you feel better."

"And in the meantime, someone

ought to do something about that plant," Fawn added.

"What do you mean, 'do something'?" Lily asked.

"Well, chop it down or pull it up. You know, get rid of it," Fawn said.

Lily gasped. Chop down a plant?

"The wasps liked those flowers," Fawn explained. "They could come back at any moment."

Lily looked at Iris. She hoped Iris would say something good about the plant. Iris's eyes were wide and her face was pale. But she didn't say anything.

Lily turned back to Beck and Fawn. "The plant is growing in my garden," she said. "I will take responsibility for it."

41

There was a long pause. Then the other fairies nodded slowly. They turned and headed back to the Home Tree.

Iris glanced back at Lily. Lily thought she looked sorry. But she couldn't say for sure.

For the next few days, Lily was very busy. Every morning, she picked armloads of lavender to hand out to the fairies of Pixie Hollow. Her leafkerchief masks were a good way to cover up the smell of the stinky flowers.

Then one morning, Lily woke with a stuffy nose. Her eyes watered and her throat itched.

"What a terrible time to catch a cold," Lily said as she climbed out of bed.

When she got to the tearoom, Lily noticed everyone in the Home Tree seemed to be sick.

"Hi, Lily," the other garden fairies said as she sat down. All the fairies had watery eyes and runny noses.

"What an awful cold everyone's got," Lily remarked as she filled her teacup.

"Oh, it's no cold," Rosetta replied as she dabbed at her nose with a rose petal. "It's that pink dust."

"Pink dust?" asked Lily.

Rosetta nodded. "It's everywhere. The cleaning-talent fairies can't get rid of it.

It makes them sneeze so much, they can't get any work done."

Suddenly, Lily had a bad feeling. "I'll be right back," she said. She hurried off to her garden.

Sure enough, her entire garden looked as if it had been covered in pink snow. When a slight breeze blew, more pink dust floated down from the flowers on the mysterious plant.

It wasn't dust, Lily realized. It was pollen. And everyone in Pixie Hollow was allergic to it!

6

By afternoon, pink pollen covered everything in Pixie Hollow.

Iris *tsk-tsked* from her spot on the toadstool. "I told you not to plant that seed without knowing anything about it," she said. She sneezed twice, then looked thoughtfully at the plant. "Still," she added, "it *is* a most extraordinary plant."

Lily frowned at her, but Iris didn't notice.

Just then, a fairy bolted into the garden. It was Vidia. And she looked furious.

"You should have uprooted that thing when it was a sprout," Vidia snarled. She tried to shake the sticky pollen from her wings. Vidia despised anything that kept her from flying fast. "If you won't cut it down, I will."

All afternoon, fairies came to Lily to complain about the plant.

Even Terence, a normally cheerful dust-talent sparrow man, looked troubled. "That pink stuff has mixed in with the fairy dust," he told Lily. "It's messing up everyone's magic."

Later, Lily found a quiet patch of clover and sat down alone. All day, not a single fairy had come to smell the roses or walk among the flowers of her garden. They had come only to complain.

Bumble saw Lily's slumped shoulders and sad expression. He flew over to her and gently bumped her arm.

But Lily didn't even smile. "Not now, Bumble," she said with a sigh.

Lily saw Iris flying towards her. She wished Iris would go away. She didn't need to hear another "I told you so."

"What a day, huh?" Iris said as she landed in front of Lily.

Lily shrugged. "All the other fairies want me to fix the plant," she said.

She glanced over at the plant. Despite its ugliness, awful smell and itchy pollen, there was something special about it.

"The thing is," Lily added, "I think there's more to it than just what we've seen."

Iris nodded. "I feel the same way." A look of alarm crossed her face as another thought occurred to her. "Do you think it could be something bad?" she asked. "After all, it's already caused so much trouble...."

Lily shook her head. "I don't think so. I always know when there's real trouble, because the plants in my garden tell me," she explained. "But since I planted that strange seed, the other plants seem as happy and healthy as ever."

Iris looked around. It was true.

The garden was bursting with colour. Even the leaves of the clover they were sitting in seemed greener and fuller than usual.

Lily sighed. "All the other fairies are so angry with me. I want the plants in my garden to make other fairies happy, not miserable."

"They make me happy," Iris said quietly. "I should have stood up for our plant that day when the wasps came. It was wrong that I didn't."

Lily looked at her.

"I like gardening with you," Iris went on. "None of the other garden fairies like to have me in their gardens."

Lily swallowed hard. She felt sorry about the times when she'd wished Iris would go away.

"I love plants as much as any garden fairy," Iris said. "But I guess it's not the same as having a garden."

Lily smiled. "You *do* have a garden," she said. "Right here." Lily tapped the cover of Iris' plant book. "Your garden is on these pages. I'll bet it has more plants than any garden in Pixie Hollow."

Now Iris smiled. For a while, the two fairies sat quietly, looking up at the strange, ugly plant.

"There is something special about that plant," Iris said at last.

"What is that?" asked Lily.

"It made us friends," Iris replied.

That night after dinner, Lily went once more to her garden. She stood for a long time looking at the mysterious plant. "Where did you come from?" she murmured. "Why are you causing so many problems?"

The wind shifted, and suddenly Lily sensed a change in the garden. The buttercups, the grass, the lavender, even the mysterious plant all seemed alert. It was as if they were waiting for something.

A raindrop fell from the sky. It landed on Lily's head. More raindrops splashed on the ground.

All around Lily, the plants began to perk up.

Lily stretched out her arms and let herself get drenched. The rain washed the pink pollen out of her hair and off her skin.

That night, Lily watched the rain from the window of her room. For the first time in days, Lily felt happy. The rain was scrubbing Pixie Hollow clean, washing all the pink pollen away.

7

The next morning, Lily awoke
with a start.

THUMP! Something banged
against her window.

Lily climbed out of bed and
crept over to see what was making
the noise.

THUMP! A yellow and black shape
threw itself against the window.

Lily quickly undid the latch.

"Bumble!" she cried as the bee flew into the room. "What are you doing here? What's wrong?"

Bumble buzzed urgently around her head. Then Lily heard a faint cry come through the open window.

"HEEEEEELP!"

Lily raced out of the Home Tree. Outside, she met up with Tinker Bell and Rani. They, too, had heard the cry.

"HEEEEEEELP!"

"It's coming from over there," said Tinker Bell.

Bumble shot off in the direction Tink had pointed. The fairies followed him.

When they got there, they saw Pell and Pluck, two harvest-talent fairies,

dangling from the branches of the mysterious plant.

"Help us!" Pell and Pluck cried.

Tink flew over and grabbed Pell's hands. She tried to pull her away from the tree. But Pell's wings seemed to be glued to the branch.

"They're stuck in sap!" Tink cried.

Lily grabbed a watering can and filled it. Then she brought it to Rani. Rani sprinkled a pinch of fairy dust on the water.

Lily and Tink carefully poured the water over Pell's wings. Slowly, the sap began to loosen.

Tink grabbed Pell's wrists and pulled again. This time, Pell's wings came free! Carefully, Tink lowered her to the ground. Then Tink and Lily freed Pluck's wings, too.

Pell and Pluck talked over one another, explaining what had happened. "We woke up early –" Pell began.

"And came down to the garden to pick raspberries –" Pluck added.

"For breakfast, you know. The cooking fairies were going to make raspberry jam."

"We were flying through the garden –"

"It was still dark out –"

"So we couldn't see anything. And I accidentally bumped against that plant."

"She got stuck!"

"I got stuck! And when Pell tried to help me, she got stuck, too!"

Tink looked at Lily. "The other fairies are going to be upset," she said.

Lily nodded. "I know."

Tink gave Lily's hand a squeeze.

Lily's heart sank. She knew Tink meant to be comforting. But Lily knew what that little squeeze meant.

The worst was still to come.

8

Rani had gone to the Home Tree to get some hot tea for Pell and Pluck. She returned with several other fairies. Ree, the fairy queen, was with them.

"What has happened?" Queen Ree asked.

The two harvest-talent fairies repeated their story.

When they were done, Vidia

pushed her way to the front of the crowd. "That vile plant has caused nothing but trouble in Pixie Hollow. It should be cut down!" she cried.

Some fairies in the crowd began to murmur, "She's right. The plant is bad. We should get rid of it."

Lily stood with her hand on the plant's stem. Her heart pounded in her chest. Tinker Bell moved over to stand beside the plant too. She folded her arms across her chest and glared at Vidia and the grumbling fairies. Then, Iris came to stand next to Lily, Tink and the plant.

"This is Lily's garden. The plant belongs to her. You can't just chop it down," Iris declared.

"That plant is a menace to all fairies!" Vidia shouted.

More fairies raised their voices in agreement.

"That plant is ugly!" cried a light-talent fairy.

Suddenly, another voice rang out above the rest.

"Fairies!"

Everyone turned to look. Queen Ree was standing with her hands on her hips. "What a disgrace. This is not how we settle a disagreement in Pixie Hollow. At noon tomorrow we will have a meeting in the courtyard of the Home Tree," said the queen.

"All fairies are to attend."

Grumbling, the groups of fairies broke up and left.

Lily flew over to Pell and Pluck. "Let me help you carry some raspberries back to the kitchen," she said.

"I think you've done enough," Pell snapped.

Lifting their chins, the two fairies turned their backs on Lily and flew away.

Lily's heart sank. No one would enjoy her garden as long as the plant was standing. But after taking care of it so lovingly, how could she bear to cut it down?

Lily spent the whole day sitting in the shade of the mysterious plant. And after a lot of thinking, she came to a decision.

"If the fairies of Pixie Hollow decide that the plant should be cut down, I must not stand in their way," Lily told herself.

Just then, Spring, a message-talent fairy, flew quickly into the garden. "I have a message from the queen," she said.

Lily nodded and waited.

"The meeting has been changed. All fairies are to meet in the courtyard at sundown," Spring explained.

Lily's eyes widened. But it wasn't only because of the message. Something strange was happening behind Spring's head. A yellow fruit the size of a gooseberry was growing from one of the plant's branches. And it seemed to be getting bigger before Lily's eyes!

I can't let Spring see this, Lily

thought. She'll tell the queen, and then the plant will be cut down for sure! Quickly, Lily jumped up. She whisked her daisy-petal sun hat off her head and hung it over the rapidly growing fruit.

Spring turned to face her.

Lily smiled innocently. "Courtyard at sundown," she repeated. "I'll be there." She was eager to get Spring out of her garden as quickly as possible.

Spring nodded. "Good. Well, I'm off. I've got to spread the message to the rest of Pixie Hollow."

Lily nodded. "Fly safely," she sang cheerily.

When Spring was gone, Lily stepped

back to look at the plant. Yellow fruits with bumpy skin were growing from all its branches. They got bigger and bigger before Lily's eyes. And, Lily noticed with dismay, uglier and uglier.

Lily glanced at the sun. It was low in the sky – almost time for the sunset meeting.

If I can keep anyone from seeing the plant before then, Lily thought, there might still be a chance to save it.

9

The sun was sinking on
the horizon as the fairies made their
way to the courtyard.

When all the fairies were present,
Queen Ree took her place before
the crowd.

"Fairies of Never Land," she declared
in her clear and noble voice, "there has
never been such a disgraceful day in
Pixie Hollow."

"The plant! The plant is the cause of the trouble!" some fairies piped up.

The queen held up a hand to quiet them. "Every fairy will have a chance to speak. Who will go first?"

"The plant belongs to Lily!" Tinker Bell called out. "She should be first."

Suddenly, Lily found herself being pushed to the front of the crowd. She took a deep breath.

"Yes, it's true," Lily said. "I planted the seed in my garden."

"What kind of plant is it?" Queen Ree asked.

Lily shook her head. "I don't know. I found the seed in the forest. I'd never seen one before."

"Lily, do you think the plant is the cause of all the trouble in Pixie Hollow?" the queen asked.

Before Lily could answer, a voice suddenly shouted, "Wait!"

Everyone turned to look as Iris flew into the courtyard. She was carrying a yellow object the size and shape of a lemon.

"Wait! Wait!" Iris cried again. She landed on the ground in front of the crowd of fairies. "Everyone, look! The plant grew fruit."

All the other fairies crowded around to see the strange fruit.

Lily saw that the bumpy, ugly skin was gone. Now it had a pearly sheen that almost seemed to glow.

"I know what it is," Iris said.

Everyone, including Lily, looked at her in surprise.

"Well," said the queen, "what is it?"

Iris smiled mysteriously. "Come with me," she said.

With Iris leading the way, all the fairies of Pixie Hollow set out for Lily's garden. Soon they saw the strange plant. The plant's branches were heavy with clusters of round, golden fruit.

"Now watch," said Iris. She flew up and grasped one of the fruits. Using all her might, she gave it a tug. The fruit came away in her arms.

Immediately, another fruit grew in place of the one she had just plucked.

Lily's hand flew to her mouth. The fairies around her gasped. Even the queen looked stunned.

"What is it?" Queen Ree asked again.

"I'll show you," Iris replied. She set the fruit on the ground and opened her book. She held up a page. On it was a drawing of a tree. Its drooping

branches were full of round, glowing fruit. The drawing was labelled 'Ever Tree' in Iris' handwriting.

"It flowers only once, then grows fruit forever and ever. That's why it's called an Ever tree," Iris explained.

"Can you eat the fruit?" the queen asked.

Iris asked Tink for her dagger. She split open the skin of the fruit she'd picked.

Inside were golden pips. Iris plucked a pip out and popped it in her mouth. "Yes," she said as honey-coloured juice dribbled down her chin. "It's delicious."

Several fairies reached for the pips.

Iris handed one to Lily. When she bit into it, it tasted like ice-cold lemonade on a hot day.

"But how did you know what it was?" Lily asked Iris.

"I heard about the Ever tree a long time ago," Iris explained. "So long ago that I'd almost forgotten about it. Of course, I drew the picture as it was described to me and wrote down everything I heard." Iris turned to Lily and smiled. "Ever trees are very fragile, you know. They need lots of care."

Everyone turned to look at Lily.

She ducked her head shyly. "Iris helped," she said simply. "We grew it together."

The fairies cheered. And they spent the rest of the night eating Ever fruit and dancing beneath the plant's branches.

Lily lay on a soft patch of moss in the corner of her garden. All day long her garden had bustled with activity as fairies dropped by to pick fruit from the Ever tree. The cooking-talent fairies needed several of the fruits to make a special dessert. The healing-talent fairies wanted to see if the fruit could be used to treat illnesses. And hungry fairies from all

the talents came by to get a snack.

Lily loved having all the visitors. But now she wanted nothing more than to relax on the moss and watch the grass grow. She had just spotted a blade of grass that needed her attention when a shrill voice interrupted her thoughts.

"Goodness, what a day!"

Lily sat up and said, "Hello, Iris."

Iris plopped down beside Lily. "I've been around to five different gardens today," she said. "All the garden fairies want me to write about their gardens."

"But don't worry, Lily," Iris went on, "I made sure to save time for you.

Now, tell me about your marigolds."
She opened to a blank leaf in her
garden book.

Lily frowned, confused. "What about
them?" she asked.

"Why, they're so golden! They

should be called *more*-igolds, don't you think?"

Iris laughed at her own joke. And this time, Lily laughed along with her.